YEARLING BOOKS/YOUNG YEARLINGS/YEARLING CLASSICS are designed especially to entertain and enlighten young people. Patricia Reilly Giff, consultant to this series, received the bachelor's degree from Marymount College. She holds the master's degree in history from St. John's University, and a Professional Diploma in Reading from Hofstra University. She was a teacher and reading consultant for many years, and is the author of numerous books for young readers.

For a complete listing of all Yearling titles,
write to Dell Readers Service,
P.O. Box 1045, South Holland, IL 60473.

Harry's Mom

Harry's Mom

Barbara Ann Porte
Illustrated by Yossi Abolafia

A Young Yearling Book

Published by
Dell Publishing
a division of
Bantam Doubleday Dell Publishing Group, Inc.
666 Fifth Avenue
New York, New York 10103

ISBN: 0-440-40362-6

Reprinted by arrangement with William Morrow & Company, Inc., on behalf of Greenwillow Books.

Printed in the United States of America

December 1990

10 9 8 7 6 5 4 3 2 1

WES

THIS BOOK IS FOR
ALEXANDRA MARIE THOMAS,
AND HER PARENTS,
JACQUELYN AND P. F. THOMAS, III
    —B. A. P.

TO MY MOTHER
    —Y. A.

I, Harry, am an orphan.

It says so in the dictionary.

ORPHAN: A person without a mother
or father, or both, is an orphan.

My mother died when I was one.

I must be an orphan.

Someone should have told me.

I show the dictionary to Eddie.

He is my best friend.

"I always thought

that orphan meant

without a mother AND a father,"

I tell Eddie.

"So did I," says Eddie.

The teacher passes by.

"Please, boys," she says.

"No whispering in class."

"We're looking up
  our spelling words,"
  says Eddie.

"It would be better,"
  says Ms. Smith,

"if you looked up your own
  and Harry looked up his."

"Yes, Ms. Smith,"
  we answer.

I walk home after school
with Eddie.

"Hi, boys," says Eddie's mom.

"I just baked raisin cookies."

His mom hands me a bag.

"Here, Harry," she says.

"You can share these
with your dad."

"Thank you," I say.

I hurry the rest of the way.

My dad will worry
if I'm late.

When I get home,

I go into my father's office.

Dr. Sol Moskowitz, Dentist,

it says on the sign on the lawn.

No one is

in his waiting room.

I knock on his door.

Pop pokes out his head.

"Yes, Harry," he says. "I am busy.

I am working on Ms. Miller's molar."

"But this is important," I say.

"To Ms. Miller," says my father,

"so is her molar."

I do not mean to, but I start to cry.

"Harry, are you sick?"

my father asks.

I shake my head, No,

even though

I am feeling worse

by the minute.

"Have a seat, Harry,"

my father says

in his doctor voice.

"I will be with you

as soon as I can."

I sit down.

Soon Ms. Miller comes
through the door.

Her mouth is stuffed with cotton.

She mumbles at me as she leaves.

I think she said,

"Hi, Harry, my how
you have grown."

Maybe she said,

"My, Harry, how high
you have grown."

It is wrong either way.

Except for Eddie,

I am the shortest in my class.

My father comes back.

He sits down next to me.

"So, Harry,

what seems to be the problem?"

"What problem?" I ask.

"Why are you crying?"

"I am not crying."

"Well, then, why are there tears?"

"I am not crying, anymore," I say.

My father waits.

"Well, you'd cry too," I say,

"if you just found out

you were an orphan."

"What orphan, Harry?"

asks my father.

He sounds surprised.

He looks around his waiting room,
as if looking for an orphan.

"Me," I shout.

"I am the orphan."

Then I tell my father
what I found out.
My father seems to think it over,
then he asks me,
"Was I in your dictionary, Harry?
Was your Aunt Rose there?
Were your Grandma and
Grandpa Moskowitz and
Grandma and Grandpa Murray?"

My father lifts my chin
so that I am facing him.
He says, "Dictionaries tell
how words are used by people.
It might be interesting
to be an orphan, Harry,
but no one I just named
would ever call you one."

That's when I remember
the cookies from Eddie's mom.
"How did you know?"
says my dad.
"Just what I wanted."
We go inside.

Pop warms up milk
to make hot chocolate
to go with raisin cookies.
I ask him to tell me
about my mom.
I have heard before,
but I want to hear again.

"Sure, Harry," he says.

"Your mom was smart,
  and very brave.
  She was a sports reporter."

"She was pretty, too," I say.
  There is a picture of my mom
  hanging in my room,
  and snapshots of her
  in our family album.

"What did Mom like to do?" I ask.

"Everything," my father answers.

"She swam, she flew,

she scuba dived.

One time she climbed a mountain.

She was a race car driver.

That was how she died,

in an accident,

when you were one."

"I wish I could remember her,"

I tell my dad.

"I wish that you could, too."

We sip hot chocolate

and eat raisin cookies.

"Harry," my father tells me,

"you are getting a mustache."

"It's just hot chocolate,"

I say, wiping my mouth.

I am starting to feel better.

"Why don't you go wash your face,"
my father says, "and take a walk?
A little fresh air would do you good.
Walk to your Aunt Rose's.
I'll call and tell her
you are on your way."

When I get there,

she and Girl

are waiting for me.

Girl is my dog.

She lives with my Aunt Rose

because my father is allergic.

"Aunt Rose," I say,

"I am not an orphan."

"I never thought you were,"
  she says.

"I have my dad," I explain.

"And me," Aunt Rose says.

"Don't forget, no matter what,
  that you have me."

"Do you remember my mom?"
I ask.

"Sure," she says.

"Was she really brave?"

"Harry," says my aunt,

"your mom once
rode an elephant, in India,
for a story she was writing.
There was nothing
that she ever wrote about,
she did not try.
One time, she dived
from an airplane in the sky."

"She must have
    had a parachute," I say.
"Well, sure, a parachute,
    but first came the jump,
    then came the chute.
    Believe me, Harry,
    it took nerve."

Aunt Rose puts

an arm around me.

"You know, Harry,

what I remember

best about your mom,

is how much she loved you.

I still can see the way

she used to hug you

and hear her call you

'Little Mister Moskowitz.'"

I take Girl for a walk.

"When I grow up,"

I tell her,

"I'm going to be like Mom."

That night, Pop and I
telephone Grandma
and Grandpa Murray
long distance.
They live in Oklahoma
on a peanut farm.
They are my mother's parents.
Pop dials, I speak.
"Hi," I say.
"It's Harry."

"Hi, Harry," they say.

"What a nice surprise.

What are you doing?"

"I'm talking to you
long distance," I say.
"I called to ask
about my mother.
What was she like
when she was my age?"

"Brave," says Grandpa.

"She was very brave.

She could hang upside down

by her knees

from a fence railing.

She rode her horse, Blackie,

bareback, facing backward.

'I'm practicing,' she used to say,

'in case I'm ever in the circus.'"

I ask what I really want to know.

"When Mom was my age,

was she anything like me?"

"Sure, Harry," Grandma says.

"Your mom was a lot like you."

"I am not *that* brave," I say.

"Your mom was not always brave,"

says Grandma.

"She was afraid of bees.

'Don't bother them

and they won't bother you,'

I used to tell her.

She didn't listen.

Your mom was smart, like you.

She liked to read a lot.

She also liked all kinds of animals.

Well, except for bees."

"Did she have a dog?"

I ask.

"Sure she had a dog.

Its name was Mulligan."

"Did she have a fish?" I ask.

My father has a goldfish.

"She had a tank of fish,"

says Grandpa,

"a turtle named Martha,

and a three-colored cat

that was lucky."

"The cat's name was Lucky?"

I ask.

"No," explains Grandma.

"It's supposed to be lucky

to pat a three-colored cat.

Don't ask me why."

"Well," Grandpa says,

"we are lucky to have Harry.

'That's some grandson,'

we always say."

My father takes the telephone
to say goodbye.
"Thank you," he tells them.
"You know I try,
but still some days
Harry really misses his mom.
Well," he says, "some days
so do I."

Pop tucks me in bed
and turns out the light.
"Good night, Harry," he says.
Then he kisses me.

The next day in school
we have to write a paragraph.
Ms. Smith says,
"Write about someone you know,
or what you want to be
when you grow up.
Put commas and periods
in all the places they should go."

I write,

My mom
was a mountain climbing,
scuba diving,
race car driver.
She was a sports reporter.
She was very brave.
When I grow up,
I am going to be like her.

51

Ms. Smith passes by.

She reads what I have written.

"Nice work, Harry," she says.

"It shows imagination,

and you put commas

in all the right places."

"Thank you," I say.

"I am not finished yet."

I write,

Maybe
I will live on a farm
in Oklahoma,
and have a horse,
like my Grandma
and Grandpa Murray.

Of course,

I will also be like my dad.

I will have a sign on my farm.

It will say,

Dr. Harry Moskowitz
DENTIST

The End